Froggy: The Beginning 2

Life In The Kooterville Swamp

BOB E. BRAZIL

Revised 2018

Written by Bob E. Brazil
Illustrations by Bob E. Brazil
Cover art and design by Bob E. Brazil

Photo of swampland in Hammond, La.

Way, way back in the Louisiana bayou is an imaginary place called the "Kooterville Swamp." This is home to all sorts of interesting wildlife and strange critters. They live and enjoy life to the absolute fullest.

Two amazing characters take the opening stage: B F Bullfrog, a large over-sized cabin-dwelling "pappy," and a little pint-sized, diaper-wearing infant named "Froggy," who was rescued and cared for by B F after a raging flood passed through the swamp and separated her from her family. Together they formed a close attachment to each other and enjoyed many good times together. But the life of Froggy is just beginning, as there are many discoveries that lie ahead for her.

And now, her story continues...

Early to rise! B F and Froggy got ready to eat breakfast.

"Mmmmm! I love milk and cereal and apples!" said Froggy.

"Me, too!" B F said. "Here is a bowl of wild berries and some juice if you want more."

After breakfast was over, B F and Froggy went into the swamp to gather some firewood, nuts, and berries.

"Why are we gathering so much wood?" asked Froggy.

"Because tonight we are going to make a big campfire and have some of my old friends over and have a good time," answered B F. "We are going to eat some really good food and listen to some live music."

"Yippee!" Froggy shouted, jumping up and down. "Who are these friends?"

"Their names are Toad and Tad," answered B F. "They are going to play some really good music for us."

"What is music?" asked Froggy.

"Music is sound that comes from a box with strings and buckets hit with sticks," answered B F.

When B F and Froggy got back to the cabin, they saw the two visitors walking toward them.

"Here they come!" shouted B F. "Toad and Tadpole, carrying their music makers."

"Howdy, B F!" called out Toad.

"Hello, Toad and Tad!" answered B F.

"And who is this little girl?" asked Toad.

"Toad and Tad, meet Froggy," said B F. "I am her new pappy. I found her in the swamp under a big pile of twigs after the big storm."

Froggy was happy to meet new friends. She could hardly wait to hear them play music on their instruments!

Later that night, they all sat down around a big campfire and ate. Toad picked up his homemade 5-string guitar while Tad set up his drums made of 2 buckets and a pot top used as a cymbal. Then they started to play some old swamp songs. When Froggy heard the music, she jumped up and danced!

"Look at her!" B F shouted. "I never saw her do that before. She really likes your music!"

Toad and Tad played some more songs. Then everyone told stories and ate some roasted corn, marshmallows, and root beer for the rest of the night.

Morning came, and B F and Froggy had breakfast. While they were sitting outside, another little creature came up to the cabin.

"Hello, I'm Kooter," said a young baby tortoise, wearing a red and white beanie cap.

"Well, hello, young fellow," B F said. "I am B F Bullfrog. And this is Froggy. I am her pappy."

Froggy was happy to meet someone her age. They soon became good friends!

Later that afternoon, B F packed a lunch basket. Then he and Froggy came to a place at the edge of the swamp where they ate lunch. Froggy was wearing a new swimsuit and was playing with a patched inner tube.

"This is really fun!" said Froggy. "And I like my new swimsuit."

* * * * * * *

Weeks passed. B F thought that Froggy should learn how to read and write.

"Froggy, how would you like some home-schooling?" asked B F. "You can even learn to spell and write your own name!"

"Yippee!" Froggy hopped up and down. "When can I start? When? When?"

"Tomorrow morning after breakfast," B F answered."

The next day B F made the cabin into a classroom. Froggy had a little desk, pencils, books, and paper.

"How do you spell 'cat'?" asked B F.

"C-a-t!" Froggy answered.

"Very good!" B F answered proudly. "What does 1 + 1 equal?"

"2!" answered Froggy eagerly.

"Very good!" B F again answered. "You are a very good student! Time for recess."

Froggy did well in reading, spelling, and writing. Next, B F started teaching her about plants. He showed her how to make a vegetable garden. Kooter helped Froggy dig rows alongside the cabin.

"I will pour water in the holes," said Kooter.

"And I will put the seeds in the holes and put dirt around them," said Froggy.

Many weeks had passed, and the seeds grew into tall plants full of ears of corn! Soon, everyone was eating corn and drinking root beer.

"Good work, Froggy and Kooter!" said B F. "We are all very proud of you for your hard work!"

The day had finally come: Froggy's graduation from home-schooling! Everyone was present and dressed up for the big moment!

B F started to make a speech:

"Froggy, on behalf of all of us here today, I, B F Bullfrog, gladly give you this diploma for your good work in home-schooling."

"Thank you, pappy," said Froggy, with a big smile on her face. "And thank you, Kooter, Mr. Toad, and Mr. Tad. I love all of you, and I will always remember you as my family and friends."

The graduation party had ended, but the fun was about to begin! Everyone gathered at a park and had a picnic. B F made some homemade ice cream and Toad made some roasted corn. Tad brought the root beer.

"Mmmm! I like ice cream!" said Froggy.

"Me, too!" said Kooter.

The food was very good. There was plenty of nuts, berries, corn, and root beer.

After everyone had finished eating, they played baseball. Toad was the pitcher. Kooter was the catcher. Tad was playing the infield. B F was the umpire. And Froggy was at bat!

"Here, batter, batter, batter," teased Toad. Froggy swung as hard as she could and hit the ball. It rolled between Toad's legs! Froggy kept running until she touched all the bases and scored. She was so happy! But, in the end, everybody won because they all had fun on Froggy's graduation day.

When they got back to the cabin, B F gave Froggy a much-needed bath. Then he wrapped her in a clean diaper and tucked her in her little bed.

"Good night, Pappy," whispered Froggy. "I really had a good time today. I love you."

"And I love you, daughter," B F answered back warmly. "I am very proud of you. Nite-nite."

Early the next day, while sweeping the cabin floor, Froggy saw a small wooden box in a corner.

"What is this box called, pappy?" Froggy asked.

"This is a box that plays music," answered B F.

"See the handle on the side? When you put one of these round records on it and turn this handle, it makes music."

B F put a record on the box, and music came out. Froggy was so surprised at the sound coming from that little box!

"May I have this dance, daughter?" B F asked, holding his hand out to her. "Put your feet on my shoes and put your arm on my sleeve. And hold my hand with your other one."

"Whee!" said Froggy. "This is fun! I like dancing and music!"

"Hey, Froggy!" said B F. "How would you like to play hide and seek? You hide, and I will try to find you."

Froggy hid in the corn stalks next to the cabin. B F followed her little footprints in the mud that led to the garden.

"Found ya!" B F called out.

19

"Pappy, swing me 'round and 'round!" said Froggy.

B F took her by her hands and turned her until her little body was in the air. Then they both fell on the ground! Now they are both tired!

"I am thirsty," said Froggy.

"Me, too," replied B F. "Let's get some root beer."

"Yippee!" Froggy shouted out.

B F made a fire, and they had supper together. Then B F made Froggy's bed.

"Pappy, would you read me a bedtime story, please?" asked Froggy.

"Sure," answered B F, as he reached for a book from the shelf.

Froggy hopped on B F's lap. Then he started to read to her.

"Once upon a time, there were three little pigs," BF began.

All was well inside the cabin. Nite-nite.

Written by
Bob E. Brazil
(Revised 10/2021)

Life in the Kooterville Swamp is fun because each person cares about, and depend upon, each other. Froggy and her friends will continue to enjoy many good times together. No chain is stronger than the love that these friends share among themselves.

Coming next...

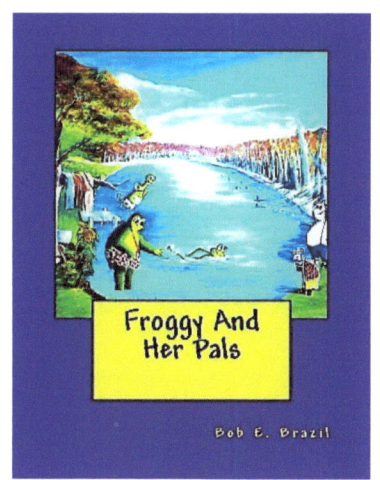 

Preview:

"Hey!" shouted Toad. "Let's have a party."

   "Good!" responded B F. "I'll get my harmonica. Toad and Tad, you go get your instruments and come back. Polly, Kooter, and Snappy will help with the food and gather wood for the fire. We will all meet back at the cabin in an hour."

"TAKE ME WITH YOU."
Brazilfroggybooks.com
Tel. (916) 342-9413

23

"McCray's Cafe" Artwork created by me depicting a scene at a once well-known hangout in Hammond, just around the corner from my house. Characters are fictitious.

Revised
10/2021

What Did You Think of Froggy: The Beginning 2?

First of all, thank you for purchasing this book, Froggy: The Beginning 2. I know you could have picked any number of books to read, but you picked this book and for that I am extremely grateful.

*I hope that it added at value and quality to your everyday life. If so, it would be really nice if you could share this book with your friends and family by posting to **Facebook** and **Twitter**.*

If you enjoyed this book and found some benefit in reading this, I'd like to hear from you and hope that you could take some time to post a review on Amazon. Your feedback and support will help this author to greatly improve his writing craft for future projects and make this book even better.

*You can follow this link to **brazilfroggybooks.com** now.*

*I want you, the reader, to know that your review is very important and so, if you'd like to **leave a review,** I would really appreciate it. I wish you all the best in your future success!*